# Mrs. Sheepy

Written by, Sydney Ortman

Illustrated by, Courtney Johnson

There once were five baby sheep who could not sleep.

Their mother, Mrs. Sheepy,
asked why they were not sleepy.

One baby sheep said, "We've been having fun all day, and now we still want to play!"

Mrs. Sheepy smiled and said,
"It's time for bed.
Close your eyes
and think sweet dreams
in your head."

Another baby sheep asked,

With heavy eyes the sheep began to count.

ONE

Mrs. Sheepy

# TWO

## Mrs. Sheepy

# THREE

## Mrs. Sheepy

# FOUR

## Mrs. Sheepy

# FIVE

Mrs. Sheepy

The baby sheep drifted softly into slumber.

Mrs. Sheepy kissed her babies goodnight and said,
"Five is my favorite number."